These stories are dedicated to Isabella and Angelina for asking me to tell them a story one night….and then another the next night, and again the night after that…..

And to my wife, Lil, for saying "I just thought you needed to have some of your own."

"…..But What *Should* I Dream About Tonight Daddy?"

Bedtime Stories that Encourage the Imagination

Written by Dean J. Vozzolo   Cover Illustration by Jordan G. Farrell

Other illustrations by Dean, Isabella and Angelina Vozzolo

".....But What *Should* I Dream About Tonight Daddy?"

"…..But What *Should* I Dream About Tonight Daddy?"
Flying

Well……that is a great question! I know sometimes dreams aren't always good. Is that why you are asking? In any case, since you ask, I'm going to do my very best to come up with something really awesome for you to dream about!

Close your eyes and take a deep breath or two. Imagine in your mind that it is a warm, sunny summer day. There's no school. Mom is at work and Dad is inside working from home. The day looks like it's going to be kind of quiet. Maybe a boring day is in store for you. You're standing in the front yard, feeling the early summer breeze on your face. You look up through the trees at the deep blue sky. Adding to the prettiness of the day, there's a couple of puffy white clouds slowly cruising through the sky.

 Instead of hanging out here at home, you think how great it would be to go to the amusement park for the day and go on all the rides. If only you could fly! Remember, though, that this

is *your* dream, so you can control it! You can do whatever you want in your dream, including fly!

You take another deep breath of warm, summer air and look up at the sky, close your eyes and, with all your might, wish yourself up, up, up into the sky. You feel the sensation of motion and a warm downward flow of air across your body that suddenly gets a little cooler. When you open your eyes, you are up in the air, just above the old, broken oak in the front yard. Your feet are brushing the leaves at the very top of the tree! "This is a little

scary!" you think to yourself and work very hard to keep yourself calm. Panicking would do no good at all. Your heart is pounding with the excitement of being up so high!

You want to see more so you put your hands above your head and wish yourself to be higher and higher. Another rush of warm air blows down over your face and you open your eyes to see you are now well above the trees. You feel frantic and almost panic! What if you fall? What if you can't get down!

Then you remember that this is *your* dream. You can control it and you can do anything you want while in it.

Below you are the treetops and the roof of your house. It looks so small from up there. You look off to the north and can just see the top of the highest ride at your favorite amusement park. That's where you want to be so you will yourself forward, holding your hand out in front of you, kind-of pointing where you want to go, feeling a little silly for a moment as a vision of movie or TV super heroes flash in your mind.

A nervous laugh escapes you, but then your determination to fly through the sky takes over and a cool breeze flows over your face and down your body as you start to fly faster and faster down the road that you live on and toward the next cross road and hang a right……wait a second! Why are you following the roads? Books you've read and movie characters sometimes say "as the crow flies". You look again at the top of the rides in the distance and start to fly straight at them, faster and faster. The thrill is almost unbearable as your speed increases so much that for a second you wish you had a speedometer like in a car! The trees and hills below you are going by so fast they are blurring in your vision. A funny memory pops into your head of how dogs love to put their head out car windows in the wind! That's how you feel!

As the park rides get closer, you can see more of them, but they are coming up so frighteningly fast that you wish yourself to slow down until you're drifting just above the tallest ride; a swing ride that goes up 400 feet! Now wish yourself to slowly drift down, down, down until you gently land on the warm pavement and take a moment to look around. Where is everyone? But once again, this is your dream and you can have anyone here that you want. I am guessing you want everyone you care about and everyone who cares about you to share in this awesome dream. The moment you have that thought, one by one your friends and family appear; your sisters and brothers (if you have any) and your best friends from school. Wait! How did that kid get there! You can just erase him or her instantly in your dream and replace him or her with another great friend from school. Now go off and enjoy your dream day on all the rides as many times as you want. There are no lines to wait in! That is what I

want you to dream about tonight! I love you! Sleep well and I'll see you in the morning!

"…..But What *Should* I Dream About Tonight Daddy?"
Let's Get Small

Let's try for a dream a little different from last night? How about this. Just like last night, you are outside on the front step. It's a warm, mid-summer day this time and again you think you are in for a boring day.

To keep yourself entertained, you look down at the sidewalk and see an ant making its way across the sidewalk until it disappears down into a crack. You wonder what it would be like to see the world from an ant's perspective. You lay down on the warm concrete, resting your chin on your hands and look into the crack just in time to see the ant scurrying over pebbles and little leaf pieces, seeds and so forth. Then, it disappears down a hole and is gone.

"I wonder what it's like down that hole" you think to yourself. You close your eyes, feeling the warm sun on your back and begin wishing with all your might that you could shrink down to ant size and go exploring down there in the ground.

All at once you feel as if you are being dragged or moved, but instead of the dragging feeling being in a single direction, as one might expect, the feeling is outward from your center….as if you are shrinking. That's because you *are* shrinking! Like we talked about, this is <u>your</u> dream and if you wish it, it comes true!

Now you find yourself standing on the edge of a huge canyon; a canyon of concrete. Down in the canyon are the sand granules you were looking at before, but from your new tiny-creature perspective, they are now huge boulders! The tiny sticks look like fallen trees and there are pieces of leaves that look to be about the size of the plywood mom and dad used last summer to build the shed.

One of the "trees" is leaning up against the side wall of the canyon so you use it to climb and slide your way down into the sidewalk crack.

Once at the bottom and your eyes adjust to the reduced light, you look around for the hole the ant went down and run over to the edge and peer down expecting to see darkness. Instead you see a warm kind of glow around everything, as if the soil itself is glowing and creating light. The tunnel is flat on the bottom and arches over where you are walking. Almost right away, there is a doorway to your left. It is carved out of the dirt and seems very solid and like it's been there awhile. Once inside, you see several rooms. There's a pleasant, earthy dirt aroma all around you. There is a kitchen made out of wood and glass and bricks made out of the soil that's all around you. There is a table to eat at and further in there is a couch and a recliner. Beyond that there is a bedroom with the most amazing king size bed with a headboard and footboard of ornately carved wood depicting all kinds of woodland creatures and birds. The carvings are the most beautiful sculptures you have ever seen so you spend a little time looking closely at them. You can see the marks where the artist scraped away the wood to bring out amazingly detailed animal figures.

On a small desk against the wall you find carving tools and a couple of plain blocks of wood. You sit down and think what you might carve into the wood from your imagination. Maybe animals of your own....or maybe an awesome new car design....or a model for a skyscraper or a fancy home that you want to have for yourself one day. In your dreams, you can do anything.

That is what I want you to dream about tonight. So, get into that amazing, huge bed with the ornately carved head and footboards and imagine yourself creating something in your dream that you might one day create for real. I love you! See you in the morning!

"…..But What *Should* I Dream About Tonight Daddy?"

Hawaii.

Dad isn't sure how to start tonight's story. "Help me out with an idea" says Dad. "Hawaii" is the answer. "I want to go there some day Daddy."

Hmm. Let's see what I can come up with for an awesome Hawaii dream!

A trip to Hawaii in real life would require you to fly in a plane to get there, but for a dream, you should "dream-fly" like you did before so you can stop and see whatever you want, whenever you want.

Close your eyes. Imagine you are out in the yard. This time it is cold and breezy. You wish the weather was warm or even hot, but unfortunately, it isn't, so you wish with all your might that you could go to Hawaii where it is almost always warm.

You feel that familiar rush of air down over your body as you start to rise up to just above the tree tops. You open your eyes and look down over your house and neighborhood and the surrounding countryside like you have dreamt about before. You put your arm out in front of you and wish yourself to fly forward, faster and faster.

The air is rushing past and you increase your speed, wondering all the while if there is a limit to how fast you can go! Hawaii is pretty far so you wish to be in some kind of capsule or something to stop the thunderous noise of the wind and then, suddenly, the rushing of the wind stops.

You are still flying, but you are in an awesome clear sphere, with a comfortable seat. You can still see everything as you fly, but now you are in a silent bubble or sphere.

You are flying over green countryside, then desert, then deep blue ocean as far as the eye can see. There are whitecaps on the ocean waves. It looks like the most beautiful painting you have ever seen!

Then off in the distance, you see some land coming up. A series of islands that look like mountain tops sticking out of the water.......mainly because they are! It's the Hawaiian Islands!

You make yourself slow down gradually until you come to a complete stop above the largest island, which is actually named "Hawaii" or the "big island". The other larger islands, in order of biggest to smallest, are Maui, Oahu, Kauai, Molokai, Lanai, and Kahoolawe.

Now that you are here, you have your wish to be somewhere warm! You can feel the heat and sun through your clear sphere so you wish it gone so you can feel and smell the tropical air for yourself. Looking down from above, you see the volcanoes that formed the island. Lava came out from the earth, cooled in the ocean and formed these amazing islands.

You bring yourself down closer and fly along the beaches just above the trees near the coast. All of a sudden something you see surprises you; black sand!

Everyone talks about "pure white sandy beaches" when they talk about their vacations, but *black* sand? You land and let the warm sand cover your feet. The sand interests you so you lay on your belly to see it closer. It looks like millions of tiny black diamonds to you. You wish yourself to be tiny again to get a better look.

Once you are tiny, the sand granules look like gigantic black glass boulders. You can see yourself in them! It's very hot so you wish yourself to be normal size again and look towards the crystal-clear water with gentle waves lapping against the sand and start walking towards the water. The hot sand feels amazing on your feet but it is so hot you start to walk faster, then run until the sand starts to feel wet and cooler and before you know it you go crashing into the water.

You wish yourself a mask and snorkel.....or maybe a scuba tank instead and flippers to swim faster! Under the surface you go, but instead of a mask and scuba tank, you are able to breath. Well, it is a dream after all!

The water feels warm and is so clear you can see the coral, small colorful tropical fish, lava rocks and ocean plants. The little fish are very curious about you and come right up to your face. They are yellow, blue, silver, red.....amazing bright colors like you never imagined before.

A flash of gold in the sand below catches your eye so you swim down to the bottom to get a better look. The sun is shining through the water making the sand glitter brightly. Something made of gold metal is poking up through the sand. You carefully reach down with two fingers to pull it from the glittering sand. It's an ancient gold coin! There might be more!

That is what I want you to dream about tonight. I love you! See you in the morning!

"…..But What *Should* I Dream About Tonight Daddy?"

Egypt

Egypt and the pyramids. Let's go there tonight in your dream!

Let's get right to it! Go outside on the deck, look up in the sky, point your arm and rocket up and away through the sky, up through the cool clouds until all you see is white cottony clouds below you. You speed up faster and faster so you can cross the thousands of miles needed to get to Egypt.

Since Egypt is so far away, you get some time while you are flying to think a little about what you most want to see when you get there, mostly the pyramids and the sphinx that you have seen so many pictures of.

As you get closer, the clouds begin to dissipate, first showing little gaps, then scattered puffy clouds, then no clouds at all. You slow your flight and begin to descend towards the beautiful country of Egypt and its vast desert sands.

The heat of the place is what you first notice. It is unbelievably dry and hot as you swoop down and fly very fast over the sands about five feet up. You are so close that a little rooster tail of sand is created behind you, almost like water behind a speeding boat. You start to come up fast on a huge sand dune and adjust your angle to head up and over the top like you were on a dirt bike or in a dune buggy.

All at once, your dream puts you in a dune buggy that you get to drive yourself! As you crest each dune, the dune buggy flies up off the ground and comes bouncing back down with all four wheels whipping up their own rooster tails of sand. The motor roars and you go up and over another giant sand dune and turn the wheel back and forth on purpose to spray huge sandy rooster tails into the air.

As you go over one more, huge dune, you catch site of the great pyramids of Egypt and the Sphynx. When you reach the foot of the largest pyramid, you stop your dune buggy and get out. The heat is oppressive. You look up the slanting side of the pyramid next to you and begin to walk up the side, made easier since the sides are so rough it's almost like walking up stairs.

About half way up, just as you start getting really tired, there is an opening large enough for you to walk in. Looking down inside you see a walkway that slopes down into the pyramid so you start to make your way inside.

As you get further in, the heat lets up and a pleasant coolness takes over. Further in, there are lights every few feet.

Strange that no one is around, but then again, your dream, your rules. Add some friends into your dream, or continue to explore on your own if you prefer.

You walk for what seems like forever, but then a door appears to you right. It has a panel on it with a security pad with an outline of a hand on it. Just for the fun of it, you put your hand on the outline. A red light scans your hand and you hear the door unlock.

You carefully walk into the room. Inside you find amazing statues and artwork. Incredibly ornate furniture, trimmed in gold is everywhere. There is a kitchen with your favorite drinks and food in case you get hungry. Further in is a bedroom with an unbelievably huge

Egyptian style king size bed with thick soft coverings and pillows.

You are quite tired from getting to Egypt so you crawl into bed, sink you head into the soft pillows and fall asleep, dreaming of the explorations in the pyramid that you will do when you wake up.

I love you. See you in the morning!

"…..But What _Should_ I Dream About Tonight Daddy?"

Arizona, Saguaro

The State of Arizona. Another hot place. Close your eyes and begin your flight! Cool air at first grows warmer and then hot!

Below you are hills and bluffs and gigantic rock formations and huge cacti with arms and sharp thorns known as the Saguaro.

Slow your flight speed down and float down to the sandy ground. You want to see the cactus up close. Looking at it is somewhat intimidating, almost scary. The thorns are very sharp. You want to touch the flesh of the cactus but the thorns are spaced just enough apart that any attempt at putting your hands there would just end in pain and the need for a bandage!

Ah….but what have we dreamed before? Since we are in the Arizona desert, let's shrink you down to the size of a small lizard.

From the bottom of the cactus, your size lets you crawl underneath the thorns like you are in a forest, but the only green is the surface of the cactus that you are walking on. The thorns point up and away from you like big dead trees, the wood all dry and rough looking. It is surprisingly beautiful in a way you didn't expect. You make your way up the cactus, higher and higher until, when you look up from the surface, you can see an amazing landscape of rocks and other cacti and desert bushes and birds and small animals and a huge hawk or eagle...uh oh! Don't those big birds of prey eat lizards? A bald eagle comes swooping down towards the cactus you are on. This isn't something you want to dream about! At the last minute, the eagle comes beak to thorn and realizes that trying to get to you is just not worth it and off it goes to find something else to eat!

Back to your view of the Arizona desert. The sun is getting low in the sky and is casting amazing shadows across the rocks and sand. The colors are all different shades of orange and red and beige. It's like the most amazing painting, but its real life! You rest for a moment and just admire the view.

Suddenly your eyes start to feel a little like closing. It's been a long, busy and fun day. It is time to get some rest.

You take a step or two and find a perfectly round hole in the side of the cactus. What an amazing perspective you get being this small! You go into the hole, most likely made by a bird and discover a surprisingly comfortable place, filled with cotton puffs and soft dry grasses and fluffy feathers. The cactus wall is wet inside, which saves a lot of desert animals from not having water during the dry months. You drink some water from a little pool, then make your way over to the soft bedding and as soon as your head touches the surface, you fall fast asleep in your soft safe bed. Love you! See you in the morning!

"…..But What *Should* I Dream About Tonight Daddy?"

Yosemite, El Capitan

Let's have a wilderness adventure tonight in your dream.

Close your eyes and imagine your body is light as a feather. There's no pressure on your body anywhere and you are floating up off the ground to fly across the countryside to Yosemite National Park in the Sierra Nevada of California.

Like we start off with most nights, you are flying through the air. The clouds are white and the sky so blue. You go up and down and swoop through the air as much or as little as you want.

When you arrive, you fly down towards the ground and fly between trees and trails through the trees and land next to a crystal-clear river.

The silence after your flight is wonderful. The only sounds are the bubbling water, birds and insects. You stand there for a few breaths, just feeling the tranquility and complete absence of noise or stress. These moments are very important in life and when you cannot have them often enough during the day, you can always have them in your dreams as you fall asleep.

Looking up and out into the distance, you see, rising out of the forest and the river is the most magnificent rock mountain you've ever seen! It has no trees or bushes growing out of it. El Capitan, they call it. That is Spanish for "The Captain" or "The Chief" and was named in 1851 by the Mariposa Battalion, a California State Militia unit. El Capitan rises up 7,569 ft off the river valley floor.

You wish yourself to be at its foot and you are instantly there. You walk to the base of the mountain and look up with your chin resting on the rock. It looks like it rises up forever. The heat from the sun radiates off the rock and you linger there a few moments enjoying the warmth.

Many rock climbers have a real-life dream to one day climb El Capitan. With that said, this is your dream tonight and you can climb El Capitan right now.

"So what!" you might think. Well, I want you to imagine you are really there. The breeze is light. You smell the trees and feel the mist from the river. Now put your arms out and close your eyes and rise up the side of the mountain. As the rock goes by, look closely. There are places in the rock where climbers have anchored themselves with ropes and hooks. You rise until you are very high, but not to the top. You find a canvas shelf, a sleeping cot, hanging off the side of the rock. Maybe a climber left it there, or maybe it is yours and you wished it there. If this were my dream, I would go with it being there because I wished it there. You land on the cot and turn around to see the most breathtaking view. You are sitting on a cloth hammock about two feet wide by six feet long with an aluminum frame. The sun is going down so you lay down. There are pillows, a blanket, some snacks and water. You look out from your cozy bed at the sunset, all gold and yellow and warm. Your eyes are heavy and you fall asleep, hanging off the side of a mountain on a cot in a very snuggly sleeping bag, dreaming of what you will do in the morning when you wake up.

I love you. Sleep well.

Made in the USA
Columbia, SC
30 April 2018